STILL LIFE

Words by **Alex London**

Pictures by **Paul O. Zelinsky**

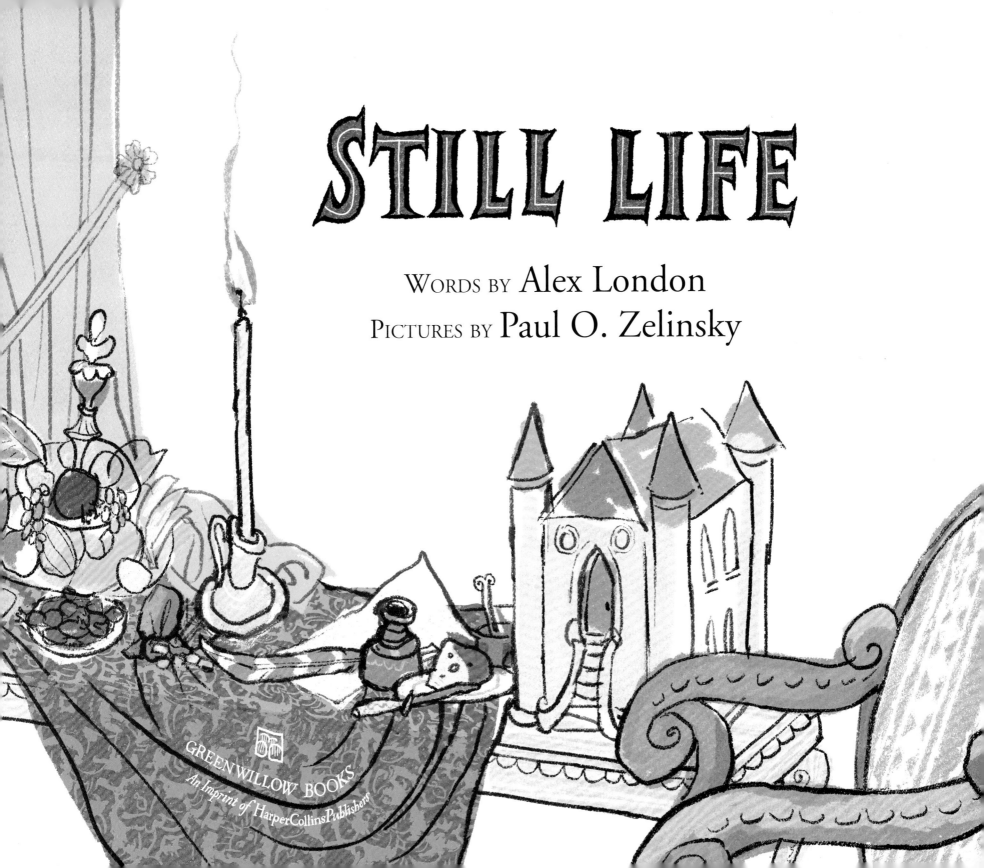

GREENWILLOW BOOKS

An Imprint of HarperCollinsPublishers

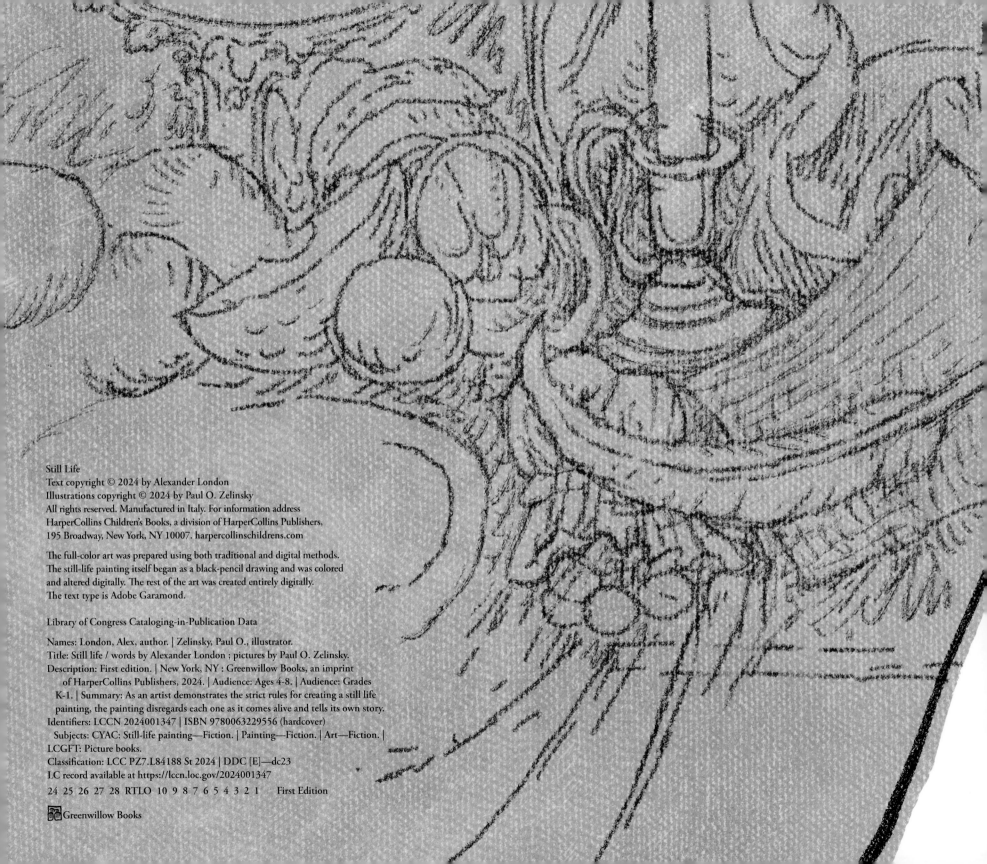

Still Life

Text copyright © 2024 by Alexander London
Illustrations copyright © 2024 by Paul O. Zelinsky
All rights reserved. Manufactured in Italy. For information address
HarperCollins Children's Books, a division of HarperCollins Publishers,
195 Broadway, New York, NY 10007. harpercollinschildrens.com

The full-color art was prepared using both traditional and digital methods.
The still-life painting itself began as a black-pencil drawing and was colored
and altered digitally. The rest of the art was created entirely digitally.
The text type is Adobe Garamond.

Library of Congress Cataloging-in-Publication Data

Names: London, Alex, author. | Zelinsky, Paul O., illustrator.
Title: Still life / words by Alexander London ; pictures by Paul O. Zelinsky.
Description: First edition. | New York, NY : Greenwillow Books, an imprint
    of HarperCollins Publishers, 2024. | Audience: Ages 4-8. | Audience: Grades
    K-1. | Summary: As an artist demonstrates the strict rules for creating a still life
    painting, the painting disregards each one as it comes alive and tells its own story.
Identifiers: LCCN 2024001347 | ISBN 9780063229556 (hardcover)
    Subjects: CYAC: Still-life painting—Fiction. | Painting—Fiction. | Art—Fiction. |
LCGFT: Picture books.
Classification: LCC PZ7.L84188 St 2024 | DDC [E]—dc23
LC record available at https://lccn.loc.gov/2024001347

24 25 26 27 28 RTLO 10 9 8 7 6 5 4 3 2 1   First Edition

Greenwillow Books

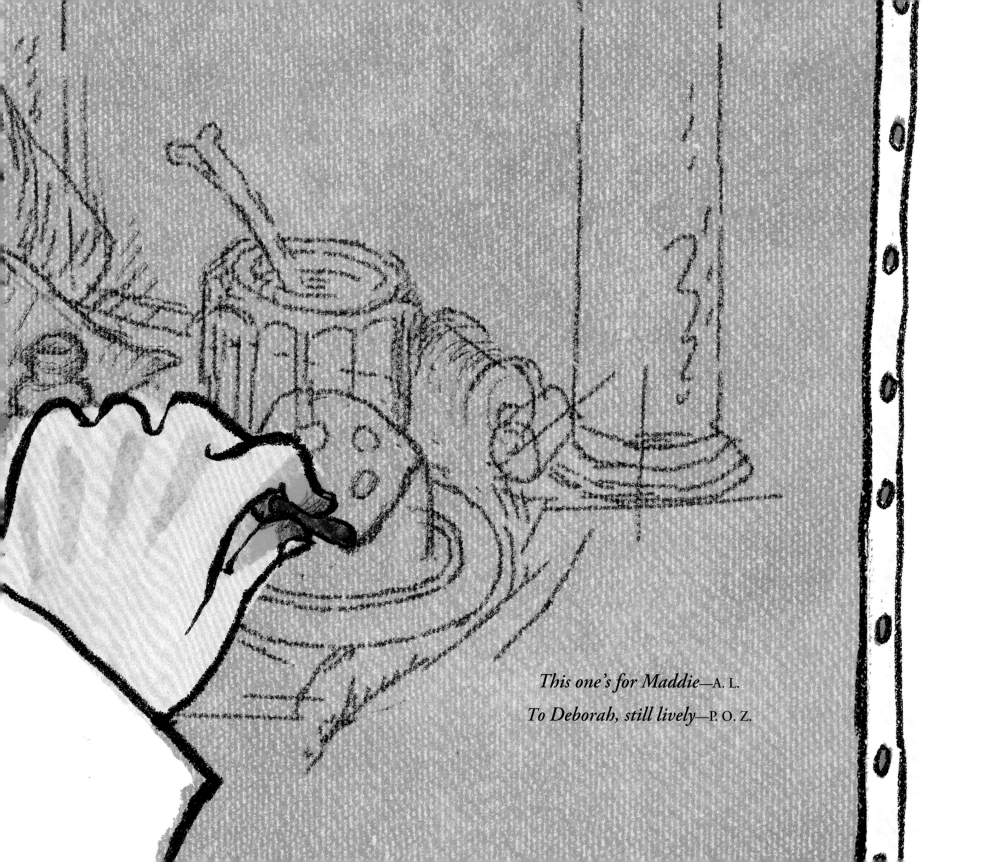

This one's for Maddie—A. L.

To Deborah, still lively—P. O. Z.

This is a still life.
It is a painting of objects
sitting still.
In a still life,
nothing moves.

The candle does not flicker, glow, or drip.
There is a knife and a spoon, but no one to use them.
The coins in the purse will stay where they are.

A still life might have a thimble
with needle and thread.
A pen and an inkwell resting
on a piece of paper.
Shadows stay where the light
throws them.
In a still life, nothing moves.

If something has bitten
a piece of cheese
and left jammy footprints behind,
one should not wonder at the footprints,
nor chase them on their winding path.
There are no eager mice hiding behind the cloth.
Not in a still-life painting.

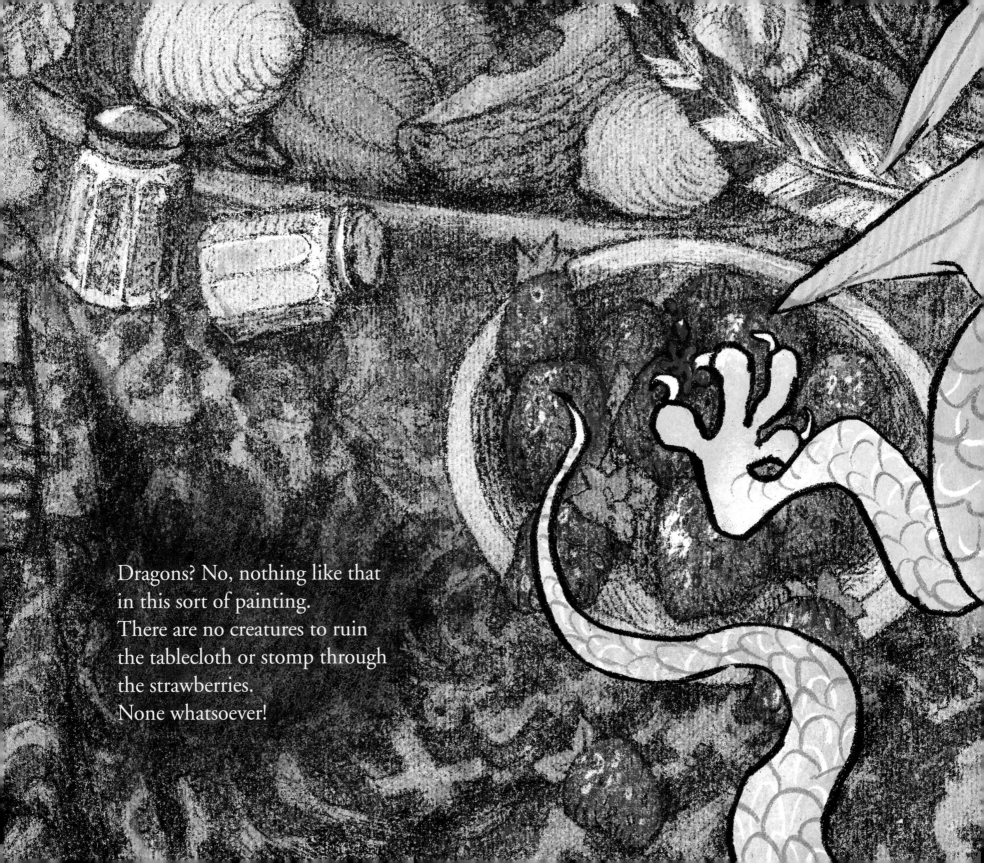

Dragons? No, nothing like that
in this sort of painting.
There are no creatures to ruin
the tablecloth or stomp through
the strawberries.
None whatsoever!

No, no, nor are there knights.
Knights do not belong
anywhere in a still life.
If there is a princess's throne,
it is empty.

The fruit in the dish stays put,
and no coins clink from
the purple purse.

A dollhouse is
a worthy subject
for a still-life painting.
The furniture is delicate
and arranged just so.
Nothing watches
from the upper floor.

If you see a note
in a still-life painting,
please do not read it.

Do not follow any clues.
In a still life, there are no clues.
What you see is all there is.
There is nothing to chase and
no one to follow.

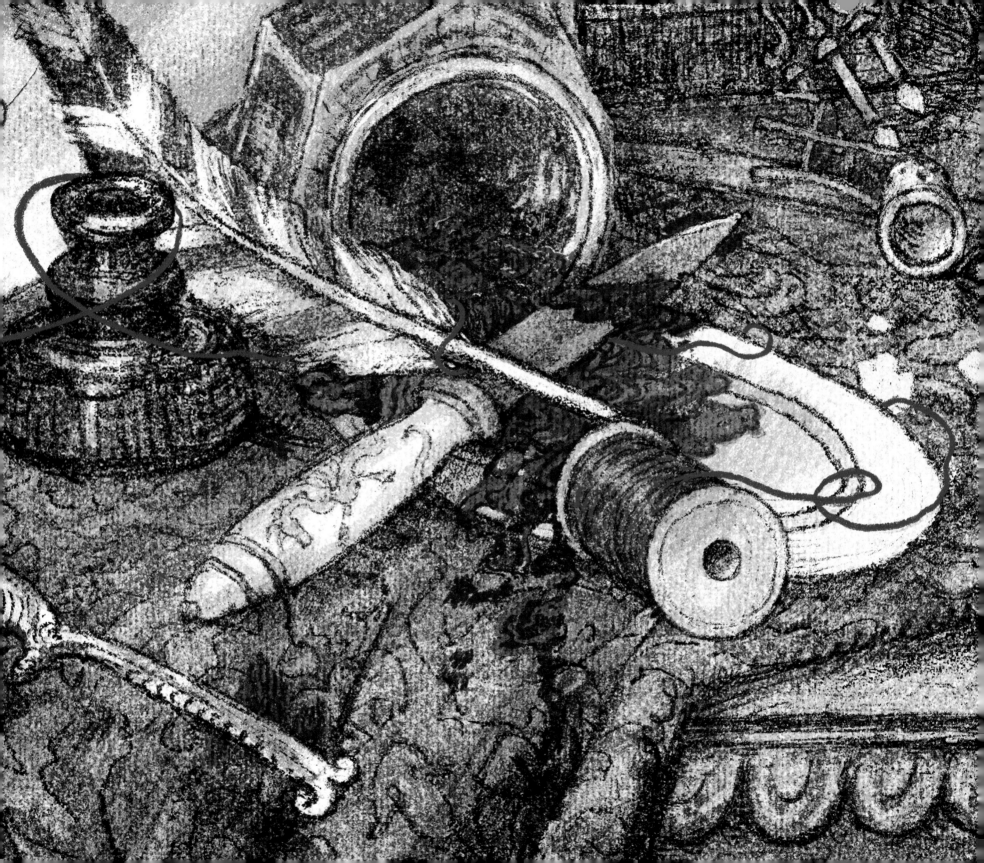

In a still life, there are no people, nor creatures, nor quests, and so there are no heroes to save the day.

A still-life painting is quiet.
No one speaks in a still-life painting.

This is a still life.
It is a painting of objects sitting still.
In a still-life painting, nothing moves.

The candle flame burns bright,
gleaming off the knife and the spoon.
The fruit shimmers on its stand.
Five shiny coins spill from the purse.
There is the thimble and the needle and thread.
There is the pen and ink and the piece of paper.
There are the berries and the jam.
There is the cheese.

This is my still-life painting.
In it you will see no movement.
You will hear no sound.

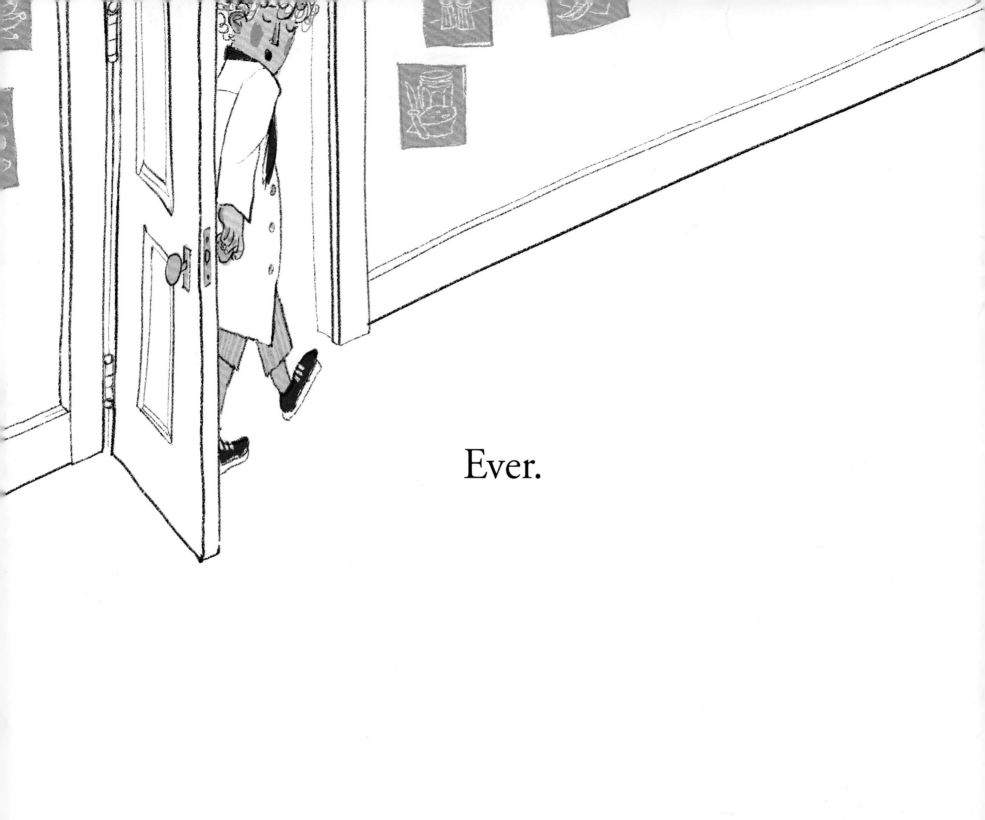

Ever.

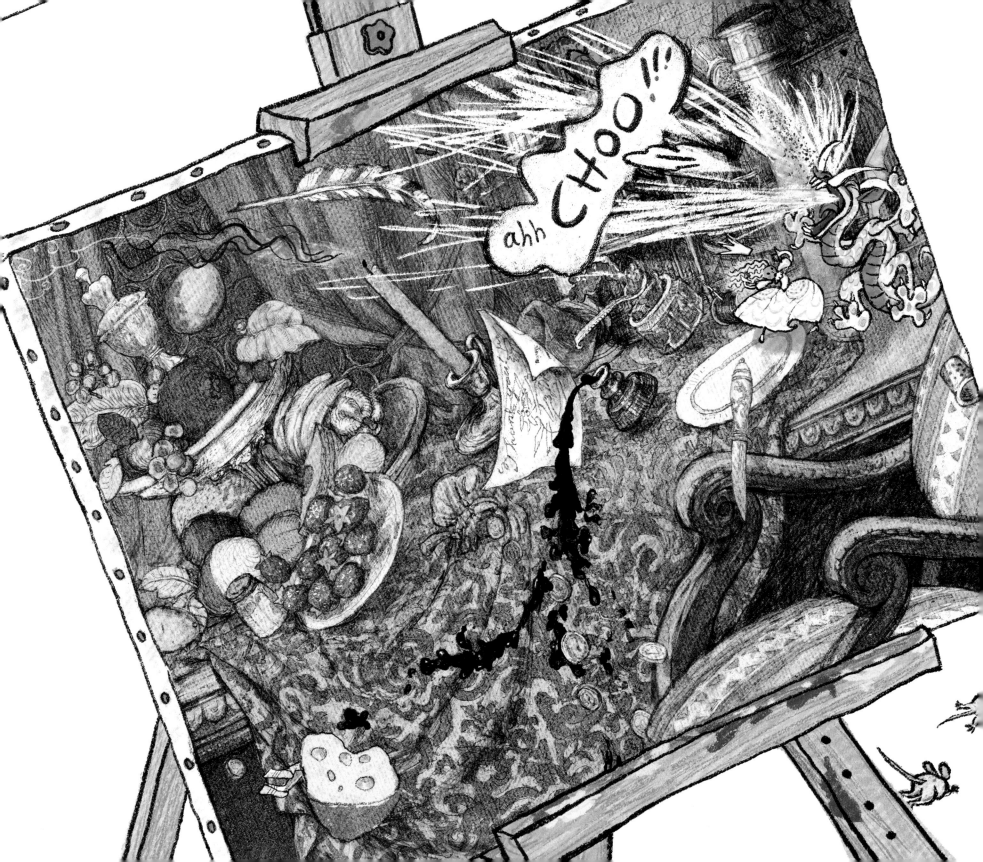